I do pray to wash away
All the dust and catch on just
Light to candle me through way,
Wisdom's bust and stars for trust,
Happiness around to ray.

Simona Prilogan

For Cristian and Cosmin, my beloved sons.

Simona Prilogan

———————————

There are no goodbyes for us

Poems

Copyright © Simona Prilogan 2024

The right of Simona Prilogan to be identified as author of this work has been asserted by her in accordance with sections 77 and 78 of the Copyright, Designs and Patents Act 1988.

All rights are reserved. No portion of this publication may be reproduced, stored in a retrieval system, or transmitted in any form or by any means, electronic, mechanical, photocopying, recording, or else, without the author's permission.

ISBN: 9798876663535

Imprint: Independently published

Cover and graphic concept: Simona Prilogan

Images stock – Pixabay

7

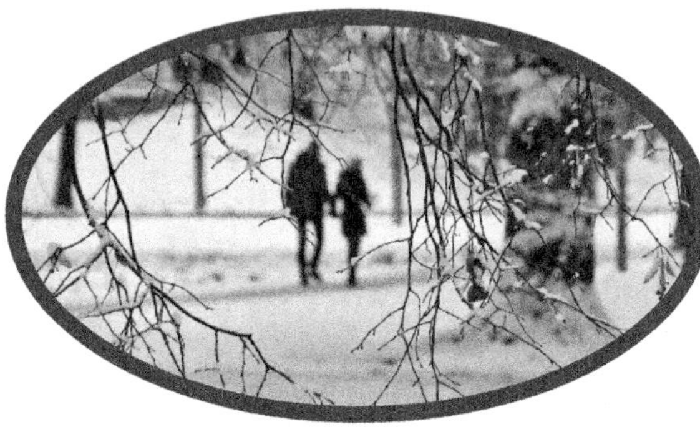

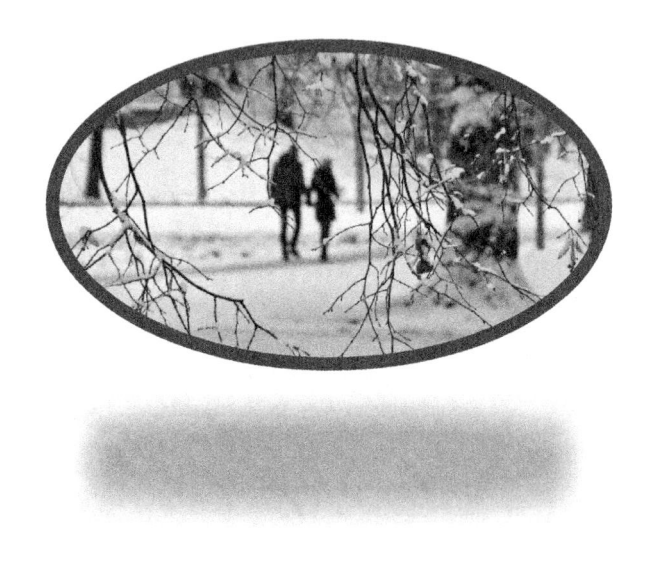

Would You Be My Valentine?

February is writing down memories of mother earth,

Covering the horizon with the snowiest fairy tales,

Bright, and cool, the splendid moon sings to sun hymns of rebirth,

Yearning warmth, peaceful and sweet, crafting hope through love's details.

In the mornings, northeast winds whisper tune from hazy skies

Caressing the bare ash trees: Would you be my Valentine?"

From ether, the psalms of joy bring the heaven close to heart,

Whitening the barren past through the miracles of times.

Turning frozen winters up to the glorious spring art,

Snowdrops smile, cheerful and bright,
listening to robins' rhymes.

Great grey shrikes are chirping songs in the quest of love skyline.

Candid days are asking nights: Would you be my Valentine?

Fieldfares, finches, cardinals, are embracing with their wings,

Seeds of hope in barren stems, penning beauty under skies.

Carrying notes from the ninth cloud with the harmony's bright strings,

Great crested grebes' excitement moves are enchanting passion's eyes.

From my frosty winter's tale, thoughts are crossing, bare, love's line,

Whispering to you my pitch: Would you be my Valentine?

Take Me on A Trip

Take me on a trip to fields

Catching purple butterflies

With the blisses' memories

At the cloudless, grand sunrise.

Take me on a trip to woods,

Rendering emotions' sense,

Gentle, magical, and cool -

On their green, bright, and intense.

Take me on a trip to moon,

Fearless steps, dreaming of blue,

Twisting a routine's fade tune,

Through the heavenly love's hue.

There is not a limit shade

But a challenge we have made,

Colouring the inner bliss

With memories' tender kiss.

Love Lane

Bright shooting stars twinkling good luck -

Around their time, we paint soft smiles.

Dusting off fate, with golden dreams,

Intense, and youthful, come unstuck.

Keepsake of heaven's timeless love.

I gasp your joy, velvety vibes

You gentle brought from seventh skies.

Reminding us of burning lust,

A nazar chants through the stardust,

Unfurling blissful tender love.

You kiss my eyes whispering rhymes

Of sacred psalms inviting peace

To shower us with blessed rain,

Holding the hands we span *Love Lane,*

Counting blue stars beneath the skies.

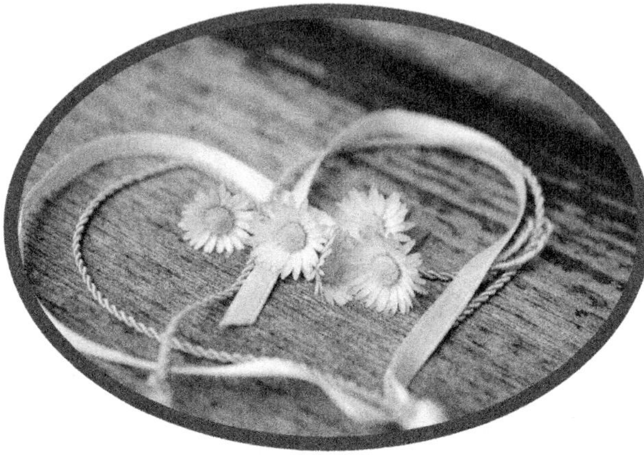

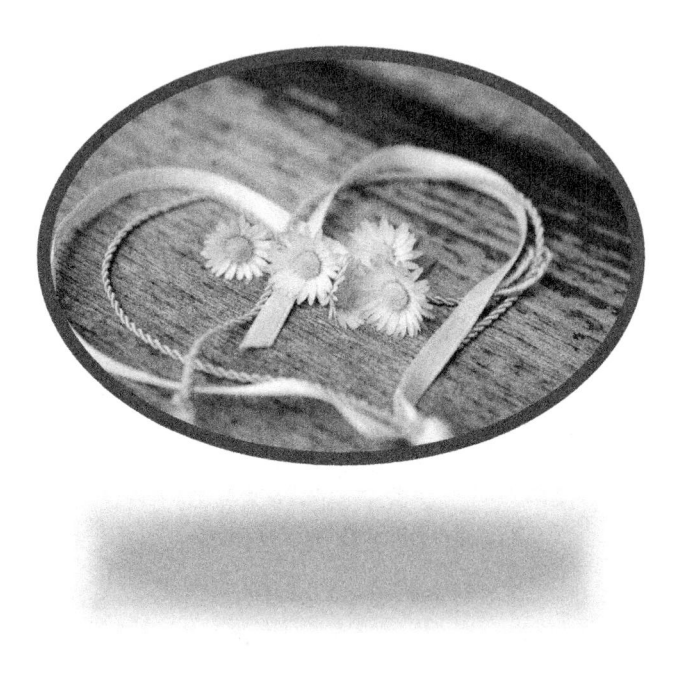

Cwtch

Comforting, loving cwtch of sun

Setting its rays beneath the blue,

Depicting love through colours' run

Ahead of magic, bright and true.

The sky drinks tea with twinkling stars

Penning soft rhymes, playing guitars

For sake of love brought from above.

Each Morning in the Sparky Meadows

Each morning in the sparky meadows,

I've dyed my pain with earthy green,

Rusty, cutting the old echoes,

Transcending vibes from the unseen.

Some smiles I've captured in the forests

Of wild unknown glinting their trees,

Twisting my inward, lasting sorrow

To scented, silky, freshly breeze.

Each dawn I've heard your gentle whisper

Brought by the playful northern zephyr,

Caressing my heart, my feelings' river,

Irrational soulful depth's treasure.

Some stories I've returned to sunsets,

Holding my hope, fiercely and tight,

Falling asleep in cold nights' outlets

Dreaming of scarlet love's insight.

Holding Hands

There was a river in my dreams

Carrying the stories of globe's heart

With sadness, sorrows in its streams

Echoing memories apart.

Yet joyful waves were kissing lands

With great compassion brought from skies

Since earth and blue were holding hands,

Shaping their trust, so bright, so wise.

There was a forest full of green

Beaming its sagas to the world

With all the burdens they have seen

Through rusty days, becoming odd.

Yet sunny rays, glowing the space,

Were blooming hopes through flowers smiles,

Enriching memories with grace

While holding hands in my dreams' tales.

There was a city full of life

Depicting kindness in my thoughts,

Transcending Eden in its drive,

Bonding the magic in love's pots.

Their reality conveyed the spark

Of remembrances in blessed psalms,

Easing their pain, lighting their dark

While holding tightly their soft palms.

I Wrapped in Heart

I wrapped in heart the golden thoughts

Uprooted from my mother race,

The smiles, the sorrows of bonds' knots,

From a togetherness' embrace.

I celebrate their grounded seeds

With love empowering the light,

Carving by grace compassion deeds

Through my whole space, so pure, so bright.

I wrapped in heart the childhood's song

With whispers of the rivers' streams,

The psalms of dawns, the mother tongue,

The forest's tunes through sunny beams.

I celebrate their feeding force

Calming my stride in stormy days,

A blessed offset in my grey course,

Holding strong stems through misty haze.

I wrapped in heart sweet remembrance

From sagas shaping my dreamland

With heroes greeting resemblance

From my beloved, sacred homeland.

I celebrate the roots I hold,

Deep, firm, ancestral, native depths,

Away from home, paths to remould,

Carrying with me their branches' strengths.

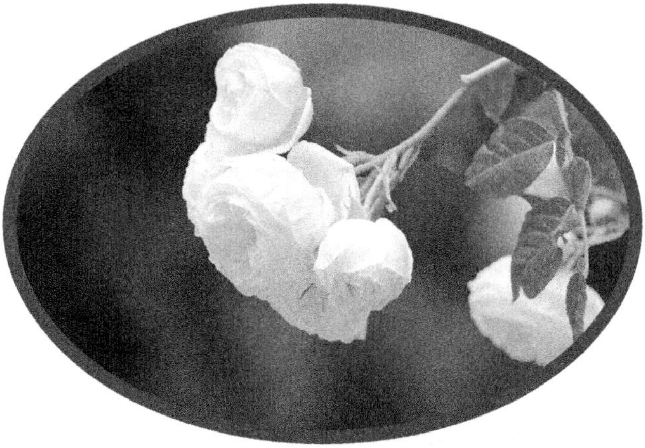

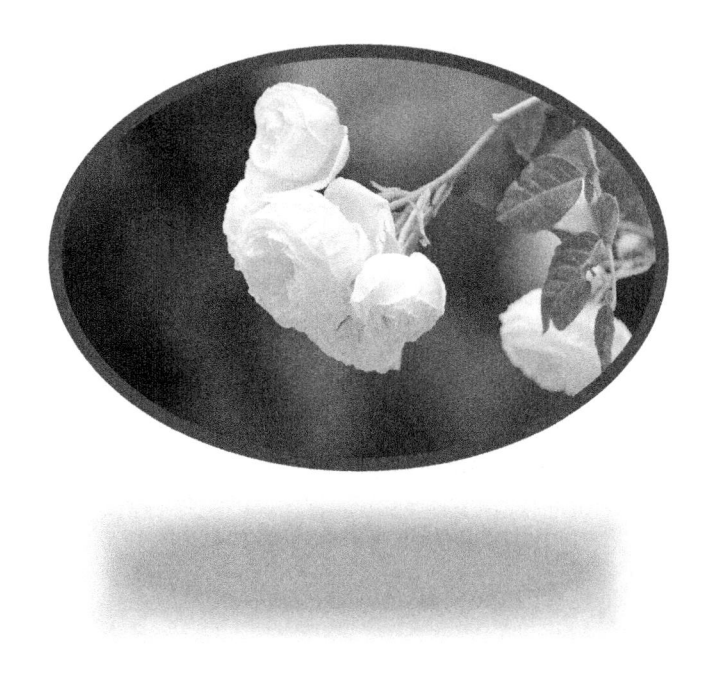

She's Awake at Night

She's awake at night, turning thoughts on mind

Scrolling back in time through emotions' spine,

Questioning herself at the manners' shelf,

Blinking eyes of quest with the greatest zest,

Trying to revive meanings of her drive,

While the hope grows dark, torturing her spark.

Stars are pouring charm in desire's arm,

Singing hymns of love rising from above,

Melting hearts despite of his leaving write.

Still, she tunes again in his waves of pain,

Bounding to his path, let alone in wrath

Unknown to unfurl in her longing twirl.

Hidden roots unfold through her broken world,

Calling a return of a mystic yearn,

Clapping hands of past, soberly, and fast,

Night is yanking pain out of life's refrain.

Rendering the sore, thoughts of evermore

Craves the beams of peace through her crying cease.

It might be a curse out of past's remorse,

Levelling the pain in a stormy rain,

Letting her to fall deep to the love's core

So, she can embrace tightly his hurt's pace,

Lightening his way to a brighter day

Through her prayers' spell out of blessings' shell.

She's awake at night, questioning her sight,

Wanting to let go, following the flow

To the silence's shore, smiling more and more,

But the shade of luck gets emotions stuck

In her head, behind of her wistful mind.

He is too apart, yet still in her heart.

God Doesn't Gamble

God doesn't gamble at the breathing gates

Neither to north, nor south behind the blue,

The strings of life are searching for their fates,

In quest of love and its balanced view.

Under the spell of happiness' green shades.

The harmony is getting pure and true.

God doesn't gamble with the fire's storms

Negotiating happiness around.

Embracing joy, the skies are crafting forms

Of willingness in search of sacred bound.

The ashes turn their pitches to strong norms

Of bringing love, the greatest nature's sound.

So Tender, So Loved, So Fragile

Your pictures are gathering thoughts, beating their rhythm on the past,

Too shrill, and distant, in my mind, yet heavy sometimes, and downcast.

Fragile is my memory now: a thin glass of old haunted house,

Unframing the stories behind, with musty melange in their rhymes.

The *why* and the *how* strode so long, twisting the colour of love,

For once it has gone in the dust, the softness has got bulky shove.

The questions were passing their trails, unstable, on wet murky days,

Letting the waters to flow, deep down in the reasoning ways.

Sometimes might be dark, yet the rain, is hugging my loneliness tight,

While waltzing together to shore, depicting new stars in the sight.

The nights are wrapping the skies with colours of hope, and with dreams,

Rendering memory's dots to mighty, abundant, peace's streams.

Still waves from the past are tuning their songs, often, calling my name,

So gently, so loved, so fragile, ahead of the sunrise's frame.

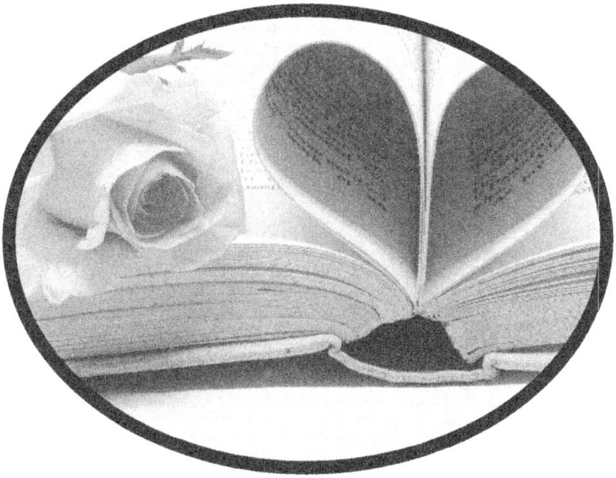

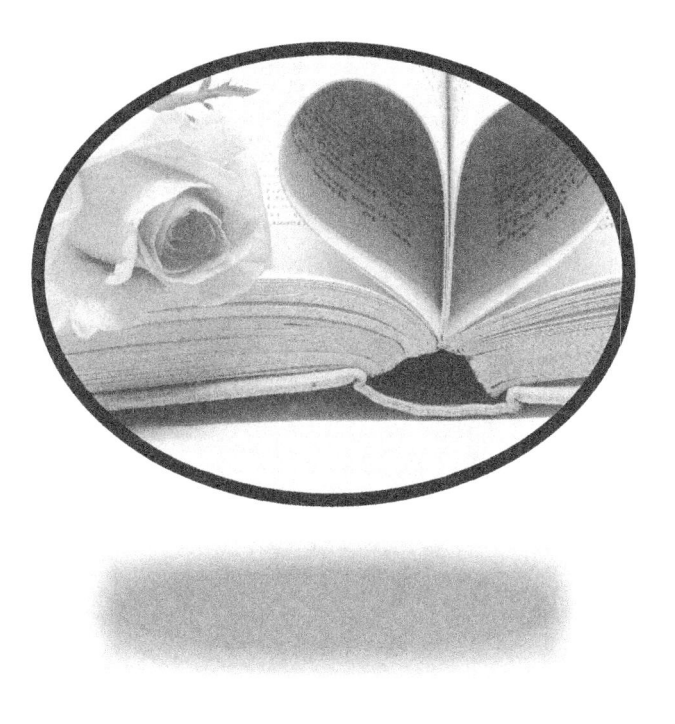

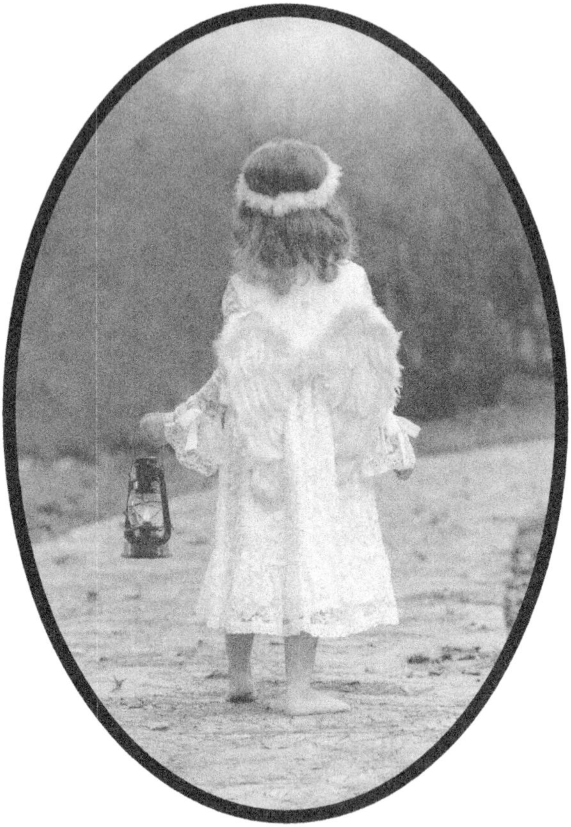

Love

Before life's shifty thunderstorm
tore up the green chapters
of humanity,
Deity intensely inked the love
on the sandstone's journal
of my heart.

There Are No Goodbyes for Us

There are no goodbyes for us

Since the rain already washed

Our tears caught in fears' clash.

Soul to soul, and heart to heart

Talking softly through blue's path,

Voicing pain and long at last,

In a sacred, inner space,

Echoing the happiness,

Tightly hugged by holy grace.

We are life, breaking the dark,

Through the mirrors of the light,

Holding tenderness in eyes.

Smile to smile, embracing faith,

Pouring feelings in days' cups.

Crafting noble endurance,

Through compassion and love's arts,

Mirroring each other's heart,

There are no goodbyes for us.

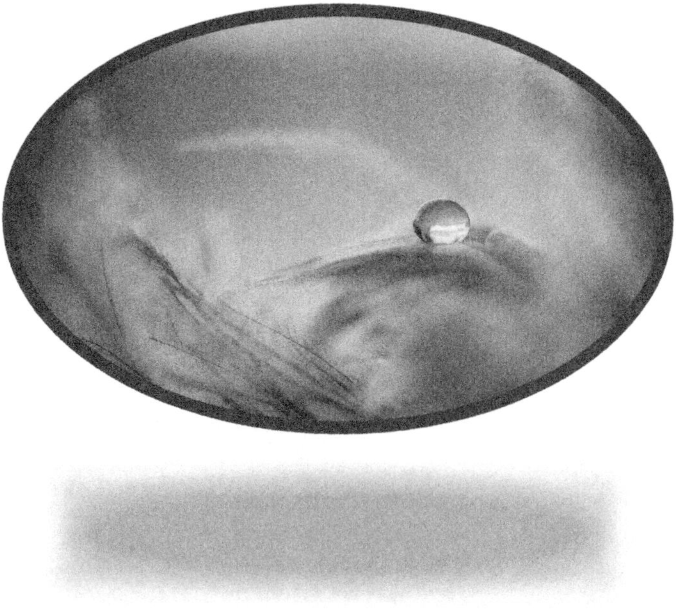

There Are Seen Angels on The Earth

It rains outside, the stream drops hope

Over my wicked paths I know,

Remembering how a full stop

Strangled my breath, not long ago.

I gasped for air, while worries set

A wild and mazy puzzle game

Unfurling the unknown sunset

Beyond my frozen, mortal frame.

Meantime on valleys of the dark,

On Friday, 13th of the month,

A nazar chanted spells of luck,

Seeking the deals of fairies runs.

Yet psalms of childhood flamed the space,

A warm hand touched my icy arm,

A soft embrace of hope and grace

Brought from above the mighty calm.

At gates of the unseen I was

For minutes, hours, trembling, numbed.

I murmured rhymes of love. A pause

Took my few steps behind the dark.

A sea of snow, a bright homeland

Reflected rays of a strange realm,

But suddenly life gave a hand:

My friend beside warming my arm.

The autumn's fears were dropping down

Their reddish masks. Bringing peace time

A choir of angels reached the town

Of my pipe dream, on heart's soft lane.

In quiet corners shadows play

Unfolding mysteries of earth.

Tackling the moon's silvery ray

A golden dawn sparks love's rebirth.

A story comes to life again,

Amazing, coherent, and true.

Aligning dreams on sunny lane

I race through hope brushing my blue.

From past soft rhymes pen present's psalms:

When winter goes, spring brings rebirth.

Whilst priceless seasons cover us

There are seen angels on the earth.

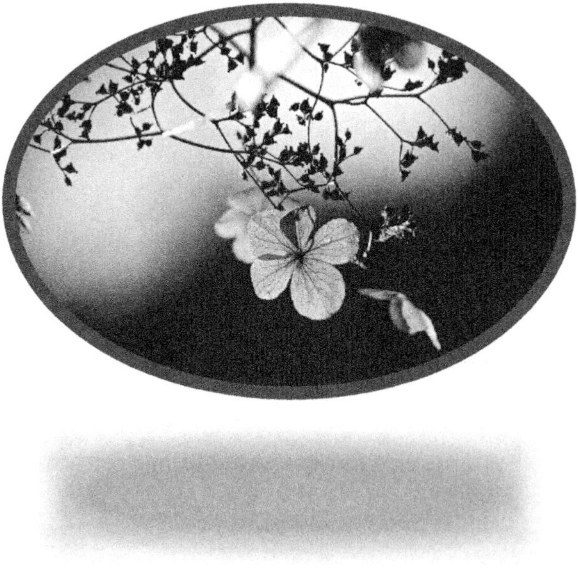

Tattered Shroud

She's hiding

The struggle, the weeping, the pain,

The ugly outward of their gain,

Her power, the motherly vibe,

The ancient roots of her tribe.

At gates of deceptions, cold nights

Are twisting the power of lights.

No longer her love's forthright game

Is spotting the bright caring frame.

The streets are yet shouting beside.

But still, she is hiding inside.

… A smile is yet left to the crowd,

Beneath of a tattered shroud.

Igniting the fire of dreams,

Her eyes are employing her means.

She's blooming.

Her struggle, her weeping, her pain,

Are flooding with force through her vein.

Yet motherly brings from above

The beauty of sacred pure love.

Let Us Play Chess

Let us play chess, Blue often says

While gathering the clouds on skies,

One for each thought, the pawn, the knight

Are finding ways through rules of life.

Let us find moves for sake of love

Despite of thunderstorm's array.

Let us draw strength from early dawns

With golden, glorious, true hues,

Shaping in seconds dreams' icons,

One for each rook with splendid views,

With hazy bishops penning ways

Unique in style through baffling maze.

Let us play games of happy cheers

With kings and queens sharing their thrones

Through wisdoms lines, away from fears,

Sculpturing life in sacred stones.

Let us bring peace from cherubs' songs,

Twisting to just the earthly wrongs.

Blessed are the ones who found their moves

Beneath the silk of kindness' light,

The greater path from angels' groves

'Till to the heart, thoughtful and right.

For sake of love, dancing its blues,

The Blue stays loyal in time's cruise.

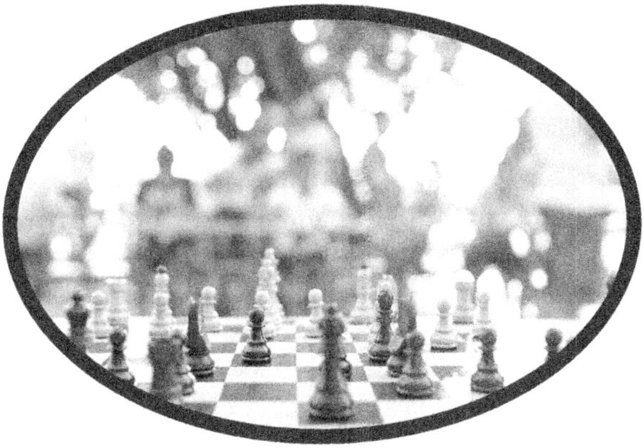

I Do Remember

I do remember golden stars

Sparking through night the zest's deep ways,

Enriching our eyes contact

With magic iridescent rays.

On cosy lake, the swans' sweet dance,

Evoking music of the grace,

Was drawing up love's country map.

I do remember colours hues

Playing Octobers' games of fall

Through crispy mornings' misty views

Waltzing their leaves on freedom's call.

On my heart's lake, waves from your smiles

Twisting to warmth the frosty miles,

Were sketching up love's country map.

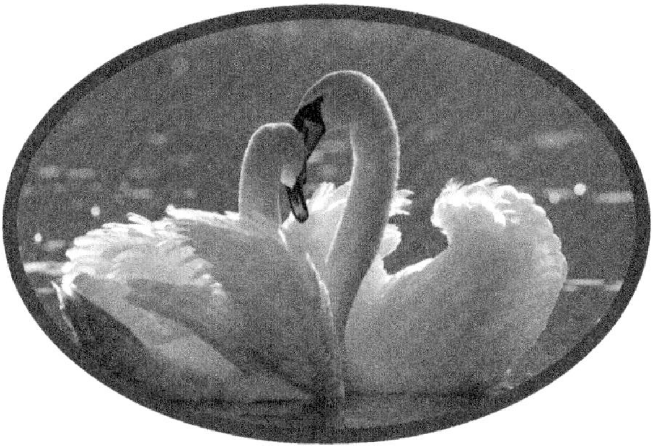

There Are Octobers

There are Octobers in my dreams,

Penning the tales on magic leaves,

Singing the tune with angels' psalms,

Rejoicing peace through Autumn's fall.

When mornings paint the heaven's arms,

There are Octobers in my soul.

There are rich colours in my thoughts,

Drawing fresh hopes at daylights' gates,

Pinning pure joy in magic knots

As golden sun life celebrates.

When earth turns fortitude to bliss,

Complete, sublime, heavenly kiss,

There are Octobers in my dreams.

My Dear October

My dear October, you have been full of dreams,

Painting my mornings through magical beams

With glorious colours embracing dank haze

With grace and surrender. A mighty, vast maze,

Unfolding the pieces of memories' pain,

Was twisting my sadness to silence's deep lane.

Writing my wishes with favourite rhymes

On golden, red leaves changing their times.

For stories to keep their remembrance heart

As richest, dense green is falling apart.

My dear October, you have been full of smiles

Waltzing sweet calmness through windy, chill miles.

Whispering wisdom in soft, gentle pace

Through golden sunrises, renaming Earth's grace.

The icy, crisp squall is hugging fall's days

Soothing frost ruptures with angels' warm gaze.

For the old sleeping tales to surrender

At the corner of misty November.

Smile To the Burdens

Smile to the burdens, my daughter. Life is not always so pink,

Not even lush, indigo, or lavender, but a crude bloodthirsty blink.

Hide your emotions, my daughter, keep them inside of your heart,

As no heart ever makes any value but tearing the freedom apart.

Bare and forgive, my dearest girl, as the Creator bares us on earth,

Praying to Him for forgiveness, weeping to Him by the dearth.

Keep your eyes on husband's delight, not even guess of your own,

As no right is granted for women but let them to suffer alone.

Mind every step you are taking, show to the people your smirk,

*Praising your spouse's achievements,
not even point out your work.*

This was the sort of mother's statement before I was ready to stage

Into blurry, cloudy life's journey, for good and for bad in a cage.

As there were no better bridges for freedom to walk in the scene

But holding my tone incredibly quiet, will make me secure and serene.

I should see how lucky I am for I'm about to get married

Since a lady without a husband is like a stray-dog perceived.

For now, the joy might beam to me in form of my child's portrait

Passing through them the full culture, the biases, the hurt, the content.

Schooling the girls to be quiet, submissively waiting for prince,

Educating the boys to behave as allowed to mess everything.

Oh, mama, I wish I could have told you, the kindness has no gender,

The love holds the equal meanings, values, confidence, and tender.

I tried to understand you, as you had hardly walked the path

Of a household abuse, holding the tears, frustration, and wrath.

Withdrawal

Hot summers – I was digging – like my ancients were turning the land,

Having as strength that motion of heart called love.

Warm air winding my face, never time to rest,

Yet I was digging, bringing out from the ground

The sweet white potatoes, and few practical questions of life.

Never look back, past is past. I lost my track in new family advice.

You better behave and do what is asked by your man.

So, I was digging... my own withdrawal,

A sort of tricky escape for my shattered mind,

Feeding my dreams with a golden, illusional light.

Rinsing the boiling mud, my eyes sparked from the past,

Like waters are carrying rich, strong memories of time,

Flowing their freedom, beneath the yellow summer sun,

Craft your luck with your hand. Digging the land

'Till hot seasons burnt the skin, let alone in the wrath

While no red remained to ignite my strong strength

Scorched under my withdrawal. And one day I run.

From freezing poignant curse, holding cutaneous scars,

All over my body and mind, painfully crushing my dreams,

Witnessing how softness is dying, bleeding its fears from the heart.

Spotting the threaten of life in the jealousy's eyes.

And so what you have been abused? That's not a reason for a run!

You won't be alright! They keep saying again and again.

Understand that women need to sacrifice!

Seeking no freedom! They call me stray dog,

Questioning my dignity, my ethics.

Digging narrow prejudices while preparing my withdrawal.

Yet I was turning a stand up in their command.

What could be even worse than that?

Finding myself a stranger in my beloved tribe.

Where never I will be *alright*.

After all those hot summers digging the land,

Bringing out from the ground the sweet white potatoes,

Learning the hard way some practical lessons of life,

I run from my withdrawal. Like a golden butterfly.

Flashback

Murky clouds were obscuring those communism's skies,

like a deadly poison the dictatorship ruled our beats

wrapping in blood the brotherhood's bread. A new tribe

was born to break the wings of humanity.

We were sitting at the table encircled by the thoughts

of colouring the future, somehow, somewhere, someday.

Yet dread sat beside us screaming its raucous tune

over my childhood peeks confusing aiming steps.

My mom calming the room with her candour and force

descending from a past tainted by scarcity's rhythms,

shifting the edge of freedom to the unseen realms,

gratefully partaking our everyday breads.

My dad welcoming serenity beneath the rivers of concerns,

togetherness in cups of love, our glorious moments,

encouraging us to find inside us the strength

of letting go those fears, seeking the utmost glance.

Like a foggy pillow, emptiness obscured hope away

yet I found inside myself the pitches of courage

written by the stars beneath the ages' skies

knowing that freedom will tune its song,

somehow, somewhere, someday.

Bond

I walked through Merchant Square these days,

Thinking of you, of our bond,

A vivid flashback sparking ways

At dreams we had, youthful, grand, fond.

We were too poor, unlucky stars,

Serving the food in the posh streets,

Arranging fruits in cosy bars

Amongst the arty concrete sheets.

Raw crabs found space in fancy plates,

Aquatic, legged, fresh starfish,

Some meat balancing tasting rates

Envisioned fullness in its dish.

Yet we were sipping our tea

From our level, basic, low,

Bending the fate under stars' sea

Letting the thrill and hope to flow.

I used to love the way we dragged

Morning routine in our cups,

We worked, we hoped, we smiled, we laughed

Reading the world between its gaps.

A wonder gleamed magic along

The flowers smiles, perhaps the bliss

Was sending rays, cosmic and strong,

And we were glad, under sun's kiss.

My Heart Is Like The Drawing Compass

My heart is like the drawing compass,

One leg stands still in my Carpathian's roots

While the other laps in huge circles

Through mother earth, so my ideas

Colour the days with the rainbow

Depicted from multiplicity's skies.

You might say that I am Romanian,

And you would be right.

My smile, my charisma, my generosity comes

To welcome you into my sphere

Where we, Romanians sketch some
historical lines

On the world table.

Ionesco, Brancusi, Eliade,

Enescu, Cioran, Racovita,

Coanda, and many others

Are some of us who chose the world

as their global citizenship.

You may benefit from their work.

In such a case I may say

that I am so proud of my Romanian origins.

Some would say that I am gipsy

because they only heard some chatter

about Romanians being gipsy,

ignoring the eyes of the knowledge.

History can teach us certain lessons

yet the amnesia may turn in a collective

where prejudices dance their belly

on the ignorance table.

My neighbourhood has been filled with arts, songs, and dance.

The gipsy boys were playing guitars and fiddles

Carving emotions at the gates of our blurry days.

The gipsy girls taught us how to shift graciously

Within music charm, depicting wonderful stories

All through ideas and emotions.

Their colourful skirts rounding circles in delight

Brought love from the gods

Straight in our hearts.

Something was mighty on their eyes,

Coming from far away.

A charm, a mystical world displayed.

From them we learnt to share

The tears, the pain, the care,

The joy, the laugh, the grace.

A sisterhood by chance.

And just name a few,

Michael Caine, Charlie Chaplin,

Elvis Presley, Pablo Picasso rooted Romani.

My feelings, my race,

my smiles in my face

Are longing the same

Allure, spark, and aim

To love and be loved.

While freedom's rhymes write

Life stories in spite

Of all our roots, colours, and shapes.

We all own the grace

From our mom earth,

Amazingly embraced

In a powerful togetherness.

My heart is like the drawing compass

One leg is standing still in my Carpathian's roots

While the other rounds in enormous hoops

Over the mother earth so my belongings

Enrich my days with rainbows

Portrayed by mind openness.

You Walked Last Night in My Dreams

"When you're happy, you enjoy the music but when you're sad, you understand the lyrics." – Frank Ocean

You walked last night in my dreams

Carrying the frock coat of sadness,

Embracing your dawns at the corner of the coffee shop,

Obsessively looking at the main street.

She's not yet back.

Unseen worlds descending from the skies

Knotting your imagination to another pipedream.

She didn't want to die...

Those mornings with pain

Were painting the yearning corridors

Up to the memory's hills

Where friends gathered the life's symphony

Playing guitars and dancing with joy.

She didn't want to go

Over the darkness' mountains

Writing the letters deep in the heart.

Pitches and notes speak wretched to the skies,

A silent breath covering the fantasy

Up to her memory's hills.

Where music rejoice was her life.

She didn't want to leave

The beauty of dreams, far from the stab

Of cutting her rhapsody in thousands bleeding pieces

Yet a refrain of soreness sung the lyrics of death

Up to the memory's hills

Of friends gathering life.

You walked last night in my dreams,

Wearing the heavy coat of the sorrow,

Grasping your mornings' routine

At the corner of the coffee shop,

Twisting your grief to new hopes.

A music of fate with strong lyrics.

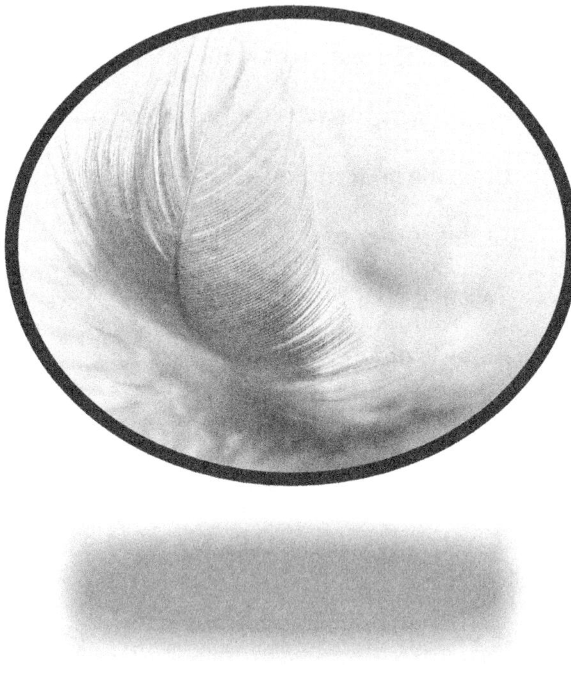

There Is A Spell In Silence's Glance

There is a spell in silence's glance,

A rounded calm conveying vow

From each of sunset – sunrise dance

Gracefully done beneath stars' glow.

Untroubled time – a haven bond

Of vivid memories and dreams,

Retrieving rhymes and rhythm of God,

While tightly folding in love's beams.

There is a spell in silence's sight:

A blue, and glorious soft light.

I Carry Stories from The Earth

I dare the square to flame my game

Outside of any wicked frame.

I see myself a dear self,

A butterfly thing-in-itself.

I carry stories from the earth,

From winter's sleep and spring's rebirth.

With colours I've enriched my dreams,

Caressing the words between the means.

From green I've gathered smiles and laugh,

Yet tears, at times, cut them in half.

But never mind any of these —

They mirror sylvan paradise:

Wide trees of life with strong, firm roots,

With wrinkly leaves, and juicy fruits.

Embraced by sunny golden beams,

And washed by mighty rainy streams.

I am my wrinkled happy skin,

A signature I've learnt to win.

A memory I bring to blue,

My depth from what I have been through.

From tenderness I've gained sweet brush

Besides the strings from grieving's touch.

They are the wisdom's merry page,

The richest velvet of my age.

I'm time reflection on days' square

Spelling love's narrative and dare

To fit my imperfections' chains

Through cheerful, human, kindly lanes.

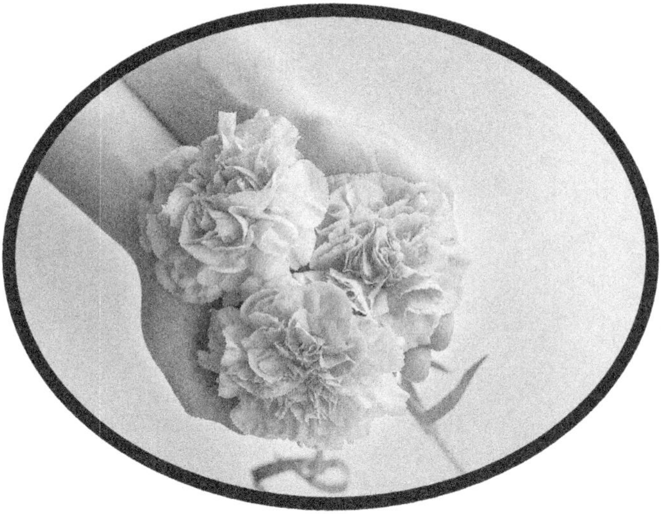

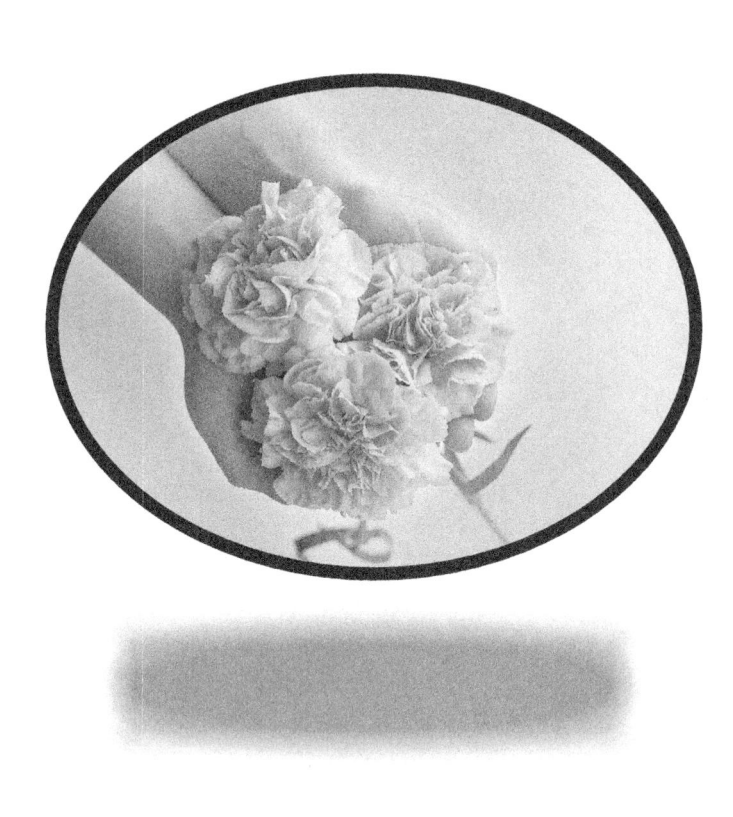

Joy

My blood is carrying soft, rhymed verse

Along these lovely, sunny days,

Aiming with force to give a sense

To the light, sweet, flowery May.

Its peace is streaming down the blue,

Bringing bright joy, intense and true,

Folding my heart in the love's rays.

Lambent Haze

I am planning, preparing, designing,

Geometric, symmetric, athletic,

Dull mornings' routines through radiant screens,

Playing, imaging, or faking

A twisted cold smirk. I'm feeling pathetic

In this daily match. I'm deeply gazing

At windows: my shirt is synthetic,

My dream is alike, a tough, pointless hike

Through diligent days, in faked painted ways.

The space twisted its shapes in truckloads of games

Geometric, symmetric, pathetic…

Feeling the vibes of new distant tribes,

A thick lambent haze confuses hope's dots

In torsional angles, puzzling chaotic thoughts,

Yet dreaming of blue with bright, sparking hue.

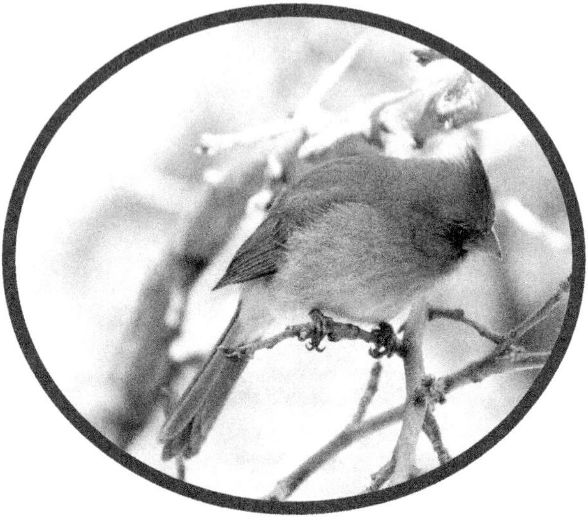

Holding The Infinite

I walk my innermost thoughts, often, with my complicated mind,

Tangled in ultimate questions and sombre bewilderments,

As bare as the ash trees, caressed by a touch of breeze,

Holding the infinite over their branches,

Twisting my ideas between the chests of miracles,

Those reddish illusions for my midwinter mornings.

Sparking joyful like the cheerful red berries on the barren stems.

Seeking the spring of hope, lost in a carousel of wonder.

I walk my very thoughts, often, with my troubled mind,

Listening the songs of quietness vibrating between the emotions

Left by the snowy spells, written in the chambers of heart.

I do not remember the season my mom told me the snowdrops' poem,

But the emotion stays with me, wrapping my consciousness in a warm coat of love,

Telling myself the legends of forgiveness and mercy,

Quiet, humble yet sublime in the shadows of seraphs

Who are chanting the psalms of renaissance written in heavens.

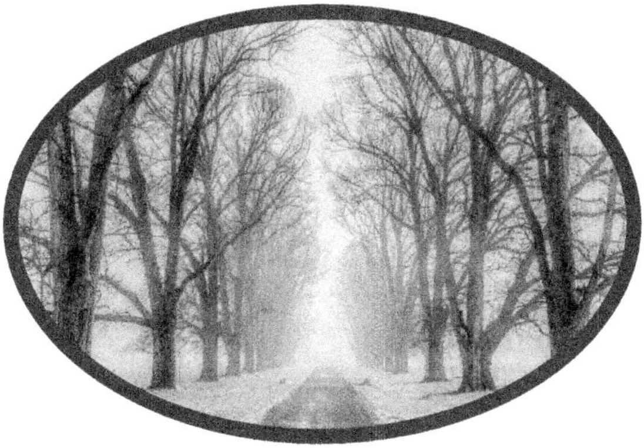

Midwinter Glimpse

Windy, chill, lonesome December, taking fascinating glimpse,

May squeeze warmth from what seems over yet is blazing underneath.

Trees embracing their sheer fortune, shuffling cards with cups of love,

May sing catchy, cheerful refrains, bringing blessings from above.

Light snowflakes may paint your windows with the secret hue of bliss

As their dance of utmost freedom breaths sweet joy upon earth's kiss.

Wild, perennial, swift rivers, carrying tales from the past's chart

May soothe down their troubled waters, rinsing worries apart.

As the breezy, cool midwinter is balancing days and nights

In a carrousel of wonders, may the peace get your soul sights.

From a rainy, windy city, pondering the friendship's smile

I am sending you best wishes for a lucky, great lifestyle

Penned with wonderful, bright colours brought by gods from the ninth sky,

While the future sets its focus, all its gates may beautify.

So, this very cheerful winter, picturing the humans' bound

Stars are sending you rich blessings: happiness may have around!

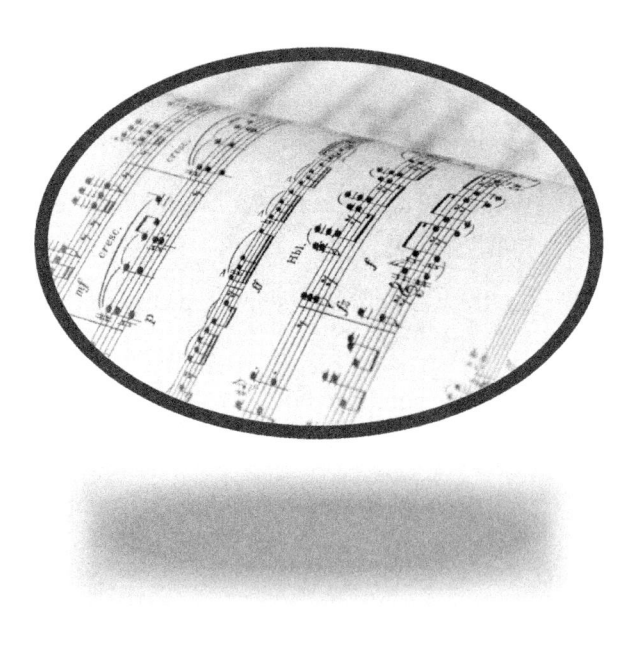
cresc.
cresc.
Hbl.

Table of Contents

Would You Be My Valentine?......................7

Take Me on A Trip..9

Love Lane 11

Cwtch 13

Each Morning in the Sparky Meadows 14

Holding Hands...16

I Wrapped in Heart 18

She's Awake at Night................................21

God Doesn't Gamble.................................24

Love 29

There Are No Goodbyes for Us.................30

There Are Seen Angels on The Earth........33

Tattered Shroud..37

Let Us Play Chess 39

I Do Remember 42

There Are Octobers...................................44

My Dear October 45

Smile To the Burdens 47

Withdrawal 50

Flashback 54

Bond 56

My Heart Is Like The Drawing Compass ...58

You Walked Last Night in My Dreams 63

There Is A Spell In Silence's Glance 67

I Carry Stories from The Earth 68

Joy 71

Lambent Haze 72

Holding The Infinite 75

Midwinter Glimpse 78

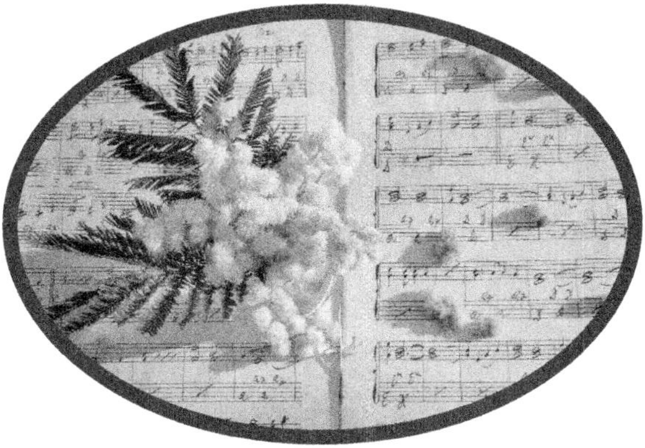

Printed in Great Britain
by Amazon